Rosemary Hellyer-Jones
and Peter Lampater

Adventure by Moonlight

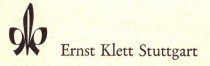 Ernst Klett Stuttgart

Contents

1. Holidays at Puffin Bay *3*
2. On the Beach *6*
3. Surprised by the Tide *9*
4. The Cave *13*
5. Figures in the Dark *18*
6. The Boat *21*
7. The Shelter *25*
8. Two Pretty Fish *29*
9. The 'Major' *34*
10. At the Dinner Table *37*
11. The Smuggler's Arms *40*

Questions about the Story *45*
Compositions *49*
Test your Grammar *50*
Vocabulary *54*

1. Auflage 1 4 3 2 1 | 1976 75 74 73

Alle Drucke dieser Auflage können im Unterricht nebeneinander benutzt werden. Die letzte Zahl bezeichnet das Jahr dieses Druckes.
© Ernst Klett Verlag, Stuttgart 1973. Alle Rechte vorbehalten.
Umschlag: Edgar Dambacher, Korb.
Zeichnungen: Karlheinz Grindler, Leinfelden.
Druck: Jaeger Druck, 672 Speyer, Korngasse 28. Printed in Germany.
ISBN 3-12-546900-7

1 Holidays at Puffin Bay

The 'Smuggler's Arms' was the name of a small hotel at Puffin Bay *, a little seaside town in Cornwall. It had been built as an inn during the seventeenth century, but now it had been modernized and made very comfortable and attractive. In the summer months the 'Smuggler's Arms' was always full, as it was the only hotel on the sea-front, and most people agreed that it was better than the other hotels in the town.

For some years the 'Smuggler's Arms' had been owned by a jovial Scotsman called Mr McTaggart, who had come to live in Cornwall, bought the old inn, and turned it into the modern hotel which it now was. The McTaggart family had been very popular and their friendly manner had made all their guests feel at home. But Mrs McTaggart had never settled in Cornwall, and had persuaded her husband to sell the hotel and return to Scotland. The present owner, Mr Wallace, an Englishman of about forty-five, had now been managing the hotel for just over six months. He was very efficient, and saw that his guests were looked after well, but some of the visitors, who had been spending their summer holidays at the 'Smuggler's Arms' regularly

* See map on inside of front and back cover

for years, were sorry that the McTaggarts had gone. They had given the hotel a homely atmosphere, and had run it for pleasure, but Mr Wallace looked on the hotel as a business, his guests as customers rather than friends. He usually came down for breakfast late, when most of the guests had already left the dining-room, and apart from at lunch-time and at dinner he did not often appear, leaving the social side of the hotel management largely to his wife. Mrs Wallace, a plump, rather untidy-looking little woman who had a smile for everyone, was quite different in appearance from her husband, a tall, erect man with a neat black moustache, who looked as if a military uniform would suit him better than the casual clothes he always wore in the hotel.

It was now the second week in August. It had been a wonderful summer so far; the sunny weather had started at the beginning of May, and since then all Mr Wallace's guests had been happy. They had had day after day of warm sunshine and blue skies.

The Johnsons and the McLarens had arrived at the 'Smuggler's Arm's on the same day. Now the second week of their holiday was nearly over. Mr and Mrs Johnson came from London, and it was their first visit to Cornwall. Their daughter Sue, and her little brother Jimmy, had persuaded them to spend their summer holidays in the South-West this year for a change. Sue, a slim, fair-haired girl of fifteen, loved Puffin Bay. As soon as she had caught the first glimpse of the sea from the car window when they arrived, she had known instinctively that this was going to be a wonderful holiday, and she had been right. Puffin Bay was the ideal place for a summer holiday. It had a beautiful sandy beach and rocky cliffs. The sea was good for bathing, especially this year, for the sunny weather had made it warmer than it normally was. And she had met Neil McLaren.

The McLarens were Scottish. They had spent their summer holidays at the 'Smuggler's Arms' several times before, so they knew Puffin Bay well. They had two sons, Neil, aged sixteen, a tall, dark-haired boy, keener on sport than on school lessons, and Bruce, a small boy of nine, who soon made friends with ten-year-old Jimmy.

The two families had met at dinner on the first evening of their holiday. Sue had noticed that apart from Neil there was nobody else of her age at the hotel just now, and she hoped that the two of them would soon be friends. Although she did not know it, Neil had seen her and her parents and brother from his bedroom window when they had arrived that afternoon, and had been looking forward to meeting her.

That had been nearly two weeks ago, and now Neil and Sue were great friends. They spent every day together. Both had brought tennis rackets with them, so they had a few games together at the local club. The two families went down to the beach together most mornings, and often all eight of them went for walks along the top of the cliffs in the afternoon or evening. Their parents even played golf together once or twice.

"Any ideas for tomorrow, Sue?" Neil asked at the dinner table one evening, three days before the end of their stay. "It looks as if the weather will be as good as ever."

"If it's like it was today," said Sue, "it'll be almost too hot for tennis. I suggest a day on the beach. Really lazy."

"All right. We'll take a picnic lunch down there, and then we can stay in the sun all day."

"Yes, good idea."

"Well, if you two are going to spend the day on the beach," said Mr Johnson, "I suggest another game of golf for the older generation. What about it, Dorothy?" he asked his wife. "Shall we try to beat those two Scottish devils this time?"

Mr McLaren laughed. "You won't have a chance, old boy! But we'll take you on all the same, won't we, Pat?"

"Don't listen to him," said Mrs McLaren to Mrs Johnson,

smiling. "We were lucky to win last time!" She looked at her younger son. "And what about you, Bruce? Will you walk round with us?"

"No thanks!" said Bruce quickly. "It's much too dull on the golf course for me. I'll stay here with Jimmy."

"We'll make a big sandcastle with a moat," said Jimmy.

At that moment Mr Wallace appeared. He stood stiffly beside the Johnsons' table.

"Everything all right, Mr Johnson?" he asked.

"Very nice dinner," said Mr Johnson. "The chef did very well tonight."

"Excellent, excellent," said Mr Wallace with a smile, and moved on to another table.

2 On the Beach

When Sue woke up next morning, she rushed to the window at once to see what the weather was like. Good! It was sunny and calm, just like yesterday. Quickly she put on shorts and a suntop over her bathing costume and ran downstairs to the dining-room, where her parents were already having breakfast.

Her mother pointed out of the window. "Look, Sue. Here come the boys. They must have been down on the beach already."

A moment later the three boys appeared in the dining-room, all with shining faces and wet hair.

"We've just been getting an extra big appetite for breakfast," said Neil. "The water's lovely and calm today."

"You haven't been for a swim already, have you?" asked Sue. "Before breakfast? Ugh, it's too early for me."

"Best time of the day, isn't it, Jimmy?" said Bruce, quite proud that he, too, had already had a swim. "We had the whole beach to ourselves."

After breakfast Sue went to the kitchen to fetch some sandwiches that the chef had prepared for them, and she and Neil went down to the beach. It was a perfect day. There were not many people there yet, and everything was very quiet. The only sounds were made by the sea gently lapping onto the sand and by a few gulls flying near the cliffs. It was quite hot already. After they had walked a little way along the beach they stopped, and Sue spread out the large bathing towel she had brought with her on the sand. She lay down, but Neil was already at the water's edge in his swimming-trunks, looking out to sea.

"If you go on like this all day, you'll turn into a fish," she called. "It's your second swim in less than an hour."

Neil ran into the water and started swimming. "I'm practising for the school swimming cup," he called. "It's in September this year, and I'd like to win it if I can!"

He swam away stronlgy, and Sue shrugged her shoulders, took a book out of her beach bag, lay back comfortably and began to read. She felt too lazy for bathing yet.

A few minutes later Bruce and Jimmy appeared with buckets and spades.

"We're going to make a giant sandcastle," said Bruce.

"Yes," said Jimmy. "It's going to have four big towers, and a moat, and a drawbridge and everything."

Neil came out of the water, and soon he was helping the two youngsters with their castle. In no time the morning was over, and Bruce and Jimmy went off to the hotel for lunch.

Sue and Neil unpacked the sandwiches and had their lunch. Soon Neil was ready for another swim.

"Come on," he shouted, running down the beach.

Sue joined him in the water. It seemed cold at first, but it was really quite warm when she got used to it. They swam out into the bay together.

"I'll race you back to the beach!" said Neil.

"All right," said Sue. "But you'd better give me a start, or I shan't have a chance."

She swam off, and after he had counted to twenty, he followed her. He had caught up with her in no time.

"That's not fair! You're doing crawl!" she cried as he passed. "I can only do breast stroke."

Neil did not answer, but swam on. When she got to the beach, he was standing on the sand, waiting for her.

"All right," she said. "You're not bad at swimming. I admit that."

He grinned, giving her a towel as she came out of the water.

"What about a walk along to the end of the beach?" he suggested at about two o'clock. "I don't know how you can sit there reading for so long. Let's take our things with us, or the tide may come in and cover them."

So they picked up their things and walked off away from the town. It was a long beach, and it was nearly an hour later when they reached the end of it. Steep cliffs rose in front of them, and black rocks jutted out of the sand at the water's edge.

"Let's walk round the end of the cliff, over those rocks," Neil suggested. "Perhaps there's another small bay on the other side."

"They look a bit slippery," said Sue, looking at the rocks. "They're covered in seaweed." She looked doubtful.

"Come on, it'll be all right," he said, and took her hand. "You won't fall if you hold on to me."

Carefully they made their way over the big rocks. They saw some lovely little rock-pools with sea anemones growing in them and small fishes swimming about. In one they even saw a crab.

"Just look!" said Sue, delighted, as they came round the end of the cliff. "Isn't it beautiful?"

A small beach of fine, silver sand lay in front of them. On three sides were cliffs, and on the fourth was the sea. Nobody else was there. It was a perfect little bay.

3 Surprised by the Tide

"What a lovely beach!" cried Sue. "I had no idea that there was a little bay like this beyond those cliffs."

"Oh, I think there are quite a few quiet little beaches like this between Puffin Bay and Starmouth," Neil said. " But you can't get to them by car, and most people are too lazy to walk all this way along the beach. But it's worth it if you do."

"It certainly is! I'm glad we've brought our things with us. We can spend the rest of the afternoon here — it's only three o'clock now."

They spread their towels out on the flat sand and sunbathed. The sun shone down strongly, and when it got too hot they ran down to the sea for a swim. "A perfect holiday!" Sue thought to herself as they came out of the water again and ran over the sand together, hand in hand.

"Isn't it time to think of going back?" she asked some time later. "The sun doesn't seem to be so strong. It must be at least half past five."

Neil took his watch out of his shorts pocket. "Only just after half past four. We can stay here a bit longer."

He put his arm across her brown back, and she closed her eyes.

A seagull cried. Sue sat up suddenly and looked at Neil. He seemed to be asleep. She touched his arm.

"Wake up, Neil! We must have fallen asleep. I'm sure it's time to go back to the hotel."

He opened his eyes. The sun had disappeared round the corner of the cliffs, and the beach was in shadow. He looked at his watch.

"Oh gosh, it must have stopped! It still says just after half past four."

"Well, it must be about seven by now, I should think, if not later," said Sue, getting up. She picked up their things, ready to go. "Come on, hurry up! We'll never be back at seven thirty for dinner now."

They ran over the sand towards the end of the cliff where they had crossed the rocks earlier in the day. Sue suddenly stopped.

"Oh no! Those rocks have disappeared — the tide's come in!"

She was right. All the rocks were now under water, and rough little waves were breaking onto the cliff.

"We're cut off! Oh Neil, whatever shall we do?"

"Perhaps we can still get round," he replied hopefully. "I'll see how deep the water is."

He walked into the sea, which soon was lapping round his waist.

"Come on, Sue! We'll swim round. It's the only way."

"But what about our towels and things? My beach bag will get wet!"

"Better leave the things, and collect them tomorrow. Come on. The tide's still coming in fast."

Throwing her bag and the towels onto a ledge on the cliff, Sue ran to follow Neil. He waited for her, and together they began to swim along the side of the cliff. As they reached the end of the cliff, they saw the tops of black rocks rising out of the water in front of them. The sea was much rougher now, and was breaking in heavy waves against the rocks. Neil knew that it would be dangerous to try to swim past them now. If he had been alone, he might have done it, but with Sue he couldn't risk it. He looked at her and saw the fear in her eyes.

"Those rocks! Oh Neil, we can't!"

"I'm afraid you're right. We'll have to go back. Don't be afraid, Sue, it'll be all right."

Sue was trembling when they reached the little bay again and came out of the water. They collected their things from the ledge and dressed hurriedly.

"Will we have to stay here all night, Neil?" asked Sue anxiously.

But Neil was worried about worse things than the possibility of spending the night in the bay. The beach was getting smaller and smaller as the tide rose. Each wave that came in covered more and more of the sand, and he guessed that at high tide the whole beach would be under water. All round the beach the cliffs rose steeply up from the sand, and he could not see any place where they might escape from the incoming waves.

"I'm afraid it looks like it, Sue," he answered, and when he looked at her, he saw from her face that she, too, had noticed how the tide was rising over the sand.

"We'll have to try and climb up the cliffs," she said, as calmly as she could. "The beach will soon be covered by the sea."

Neil was silent. In the fading light he was trying hard to see some way up the cliffs, but wherever he looked they seemed steep and dangerous. He guessed they were at least sixty feet high.

Suddenly Sue pointed to a place about half-way up.

"Isn't that some sort of path?"

The both stared upwards. They could just see a rough path, narrow and overgrown with weeds, leading up the cliff in a zig-zag. But it seemed impossible to get to it from the beach itself, as it started about ten or twelve feet above the sand. Pieces of broken rock, which lay on the beach, showed that the path had once led all the way down to the sand, but had now fallen away.

"We must get up there somehow!" said Neil, trying not to show that he was beginning to feel a little afraid. The waves were only a few yards away from the top of the beach now; they hadn't much time. He looked at the face of the cliff carefully. Yes, he thought he could climb up to the path all right. But what about Sue?

"I'll go first."

Carefully he started to climb upwards; the cliff was firmer than he had dared to hope, and his feet and hands quickly found a hold. Soon he reached the ledge where the path began. He looked down at Sue.

"It's not so bad as it looks! Try to come up the same way as I did. The cliff's quite firm."

Trembling a little, Sue followed. She moved very slowly, always afraid that she might slip. But at last she was high enough to take hold of Neil's hand as he leaned over from the path to help her. A moment later she had joined him on the ledge.

"All right?" he asked.

She nodded.

"Well done. Now let's see how far we can get up this path. If it gets dangerous, we shan't go on, so you needn't worry. We're high enough now to be safe from the sea."

Sue held his hand tightly as they climbed up the path. It was very narrow and uneven, and in parts it had broken away. It looked as if nobody had used it for years. Sue was afraid to look down at the beach, and kept her eyes on the cliff face. They turned the first corner of the zig-zag and at once the path became wider.

"Look!" said Neil suddenly. "A cave!"

4 The Cave

They now stood on a wide ledge. To their left the cliff dropped steeply down to the beach, and to their right they saw a large dark hole in the cliff face — a cave.

"Let's have a look at it," said Neil, and they went over to the mouth of the cave and looked inside. Everything was rather dark, and it was difficult to see exactly how large it was. The roof, which was quite high at the entrance, sloped gradually down into the blackness further in. The floor was uneven; here and there lay a few rocks.

"What about waiting in here until the tide goes out?" Sue suggested. "It would be better than climbing the rest of the way up the cliff."

"I'd rather go on if we can," said Neil. "Come on, let's see just what the path looks like higher up."

They went out onto the ledge and looked up the cliff face. They were about half-way up now. The zig-zag of the path above them looked narrow and difficult to climb. Sue shook her head.

"It's too dangerous. I don't think we ought to try it. If your foot slipped on a stone up there, you'd fall straight down the cliff face. It's very steep, and there aren't even any bushes to catch you if you fell."

"All right then. Let's go back to the cave."

Neil felt disappointed. If he had been alone, he would have gone up the path to the cliff top. He didn't think it was as dangerous as Sue said. But he couldn't leave her here alone, and he could see that it was no good trying to persuade her to come with him. They would have to stay in the cave, and go back over the rocks again when the tide was low enough.

"We'll have at least three hours to wait, Sue. It must have been low tide when we came over the rocks this afternoon at three. That means it won't be low tide again until after three o'clock tomorrow morning. I don't think we'll be able to get round there safely before midnight — at the earliest. And it must be about nine o'clock now."

In the last ten minutes it had become much darker. Gathering clouds had shortened the evening, and night was quickly taking its place. Already the colour of the sea was changing from blue to black, and the outlines of the cliffs around the little bay were no longer clear.

They sat down together on a flat rock at the mouth of the cave and looked out towards the sea. Nothing could be seen of the beach from where they were sitting, as the cave itself was well set back from the lower part of the cliff face. It was no wonder they had not seen the cave from below; nobody looking up at the cliffs from the beach could possibly guess that a cave was there, hidden at the back of that ledge half-way up.

"Heaven knows what our parents will think when we don't come back this evening," said Sue. "I hope they don't worry too much."

Neil smiled. "Perhaps they'll think we've eloped!"

"Oh, people don't elope nowadays," Sue teased. "They simply —"

"Shh!" Neil's hand tightened on Sue's shoulder. "What was that noise?" he whispered.

They both listened. They could hear the sound of the waves breaking rhythmically onto the bottom of the cliff below.

"Only the sea," said Sue quietly.

But then they both heard quite a different noise. Footsteps! The sound of someone walking over the loose stones of the cliff path was coming nearer. Suddenly afraid, Sue clung to Neil for protection, though she did not know why.

Who could it be, coming down the lonely the cliff path in the darkness? Could someone be coming to look for them? Neil wondered. But how could anyone have guessed that they were there?

The footsteps came nearer and a beam of yellow light suddenly flashed onto the ground in front of the cave entrance. The tall figure of a man appeared, a torch in his hand. He stopped.

The light of the torch flashed from Neil to Sue, blinding them for a moment. Then there was a laugh.

"Well, what's this? Found my cave, have you? Well, I never thought I'd have company in here tonight, I must say! But it's a funny time of day to be out enjoying the sea air, isn't it? Though I suppose at your age..."

"But who are you? What are you doing here?" Neil said as the man sat down beside him. It was most mysterious.

The man laughed again. "You speak as if I had no business to be here at all! Well, if you're interested, I'll tell you."

He shone the torch away from their faces, and in the dim light they could see something of his appearance. A young man of about twenty, with untidy curly hair and rough clothes, was what they saw.

"My name's Dave. I'm just an ordinary student. University. My subject's biology, and I've come down to Cornwall to have a look at some of the wild-life around the coast here. I've been here about a week now."

"And you sleep in this cave?" asked Sue, relieved that the mysterious stranger should have turned out to be so harmless after all.

"Yes, I spend most of the day out on the cliff top, or down on the lonely little beaches round here. You'd never believe some of the things I've seen. Those beaches, at least some of them, are like virgin country — nobody ever goes there. Except me, of course! Well, anyway, when it gets dark, I come down here to this little cave. I expect you've seen my things."

"No, we haven't" said Neil. "We've only been here a few

minutes, and when we came it was too dark to see anything much in here."

"Well, I've got my air-bed and sleeping-bag at the back there. And my supply of food – mostly tins, actually." He flashed the torch into the back of the cave to show them. "But what about you? How did you two get here?"

They told him.

"Well, you'll be lucky if you get past those rocks again before two o'clock. But I shouldn't try it at night if I were you. You'd never see your way down the cliff. Better wait till it's light. It gets light pretty early in the mornings still – it's only the beginning of August."

"What about the cliff path?" asked Neil, who would have liked to climb up the rest of the way, even now.

"The top part's a bit tricky. I've nearly slipped up there myself, once or twice. You've got to be careful – if you fell off the path, you'd be lucky to escape with a broken leg. No, I'd go back the way you came if I were you."

He got up and went to the back of the cave.

"You're hungry, I expect, aren't you? Come and share my meagre supper! It's not up to much, I admit, but you're welcome to have some. I've got a little camp-stove. We'll put it out there at the entrance."

The three of them were, soon sitting in front of the small stove, eating sausages and hunks of bread. Dave fetched a couple of cans of beer for himself and Neil, and offered Sue some lemonade.

"However did you manage to get all these things up here?" she asked.

"Oh, I didn't bring everything at once. Most days I buy a few things and bring them up with me. The worst part's at the bottom, of course, where the path has fallen away, but I just throw the things up onto the ledge from the beach if I'm coming that way, and the rest is quite easy."

Dave was an interesting companion, and the time went quickly. Luckily the night was warm, and they were sheltered from the wind, so even Sue, who was usually the first to feel the cold, was happy enough in her thin beach clothes. She was beginning to enjoy their adventure, looking forward to telling her friends about it when she returned to school. They would be quite envious! Dreamily she gazed out to sea.

And then, quite suddenly, she saw a light. Far away, out on the water. Just a sudden flash. And then darkness. And a moment later another flash.

"I wonder what that is. That light out there, I mean. Could it be a lighthouse?"

"A light?" said Dave, surprised. "No, there isn't a lighthouse for miles around." He looked at the flashing light on the sea. "It's the first time I've seen anything like that here. It must be a boat."

"But why the flashing light?" Sue asked.

"Perhaps it's a signal," suggested Neil. "You know, morse or something."

"Don't be silly," Sue laughed. "Morse! What an idea! You'll be saying it's a boat full of smugglers next!"

"Well, it might be," said Neil, who didn't like of be made fun of. "After all, it would be an ideal place for smugglers here, wouldn't it?"

He got up and looked out from the ledge in front of the cave.

"There's another light up there!" he cried in excitement.

"Where?" said Dave, getting up too.

"On the cliff top, I think. Come and see."

Dave and Sue joined him, and he pointed up in the direction of the cliff top at the far end of the little bay. There, another light flashed. Then it stopped, and flashed again.

"Yes, I think it's morse all right," said Dave. "Someone's answering that signal."

5 Figures in the Dark

The light on the cliff top continued to flash for a few moments. Then it stopped and there was darkness again everywhere. Nothing more was to be seen of the light out at sea.

"What a pity we couldn't understand what the signals were about," said Sue. "Don't either of you know morse code?"

Dave and Neil shook their heads.

"The only thing I remember of it is the SOS signal," said Dave, "but that's no good to us now."

"Well, I feel pretty sure they're smugglers," said Neil eagerly. "Who else would come out here to the cliff top at this time and make signals to a boat out at sea?"

"We've a good chance of finding out, anyway," said Dave, who was also becoming interested in the possible meaning of the strange goings-on. "If they are smugglers, the boat will probably land here somewhere to deliver the goods – or collect them, depending on what they're up to. If they land in this little bay, we'll see what's going on."

They sat at the cave entrance and waited to see if anything would happen. The sky, which had clouded over in the evening, was dark, and the dim shape of the moon could be seen now and then behind the slowly moving clouds. Nothing could be seen of the boat from which the first signals had presumably come.

"I think the clouds are thinning out a bit," said Neil at last. "If the moon comes out, we might see something."

Just after he had spoken, the moon actually appeared from behind the clouds. It cast a thin, cold light on the water.

"There it is!" cried Sue suddenly. "That must be the boat."

They all stared out to sea. Still quite far away, a small rowing boat could just be seen on the water. It was slowly moving towards the bay. Clouds covered the moon again for a few minutes, and they could see nothing more. When the moon reappeared, the boat had come much nearer to the shore. They could just make out two dark figures in the boat.

"They're going to land here, that's certain!" said Neil in excitement. "They're getting near now, so let's keep quiet!"

In a moment the sound of the oars working through the water could be heard, and then, when they had landed, the noise of the boat being pulled up the narrow strip of sand below the cliff which the tide, now going out, had uncovered.

"You don't think they're going to climb up the cliff path, do you?" asked Sue in an uneasy whisper.

"It's the only way to reach the cliff top from the beach," said Dave quietly. "Yes, they'll come past the cave all right."

"Let's move further in!" Sue insisted. "We don't want to be seen. If they're smugglers, they might be dangerous."

All three went quietly to the back of the cave and sat on Dave's air-bed, waiting in suspense for the men to appear. It was not long before they heard footsteps and the sound of voices. The men were coming up the cliff path. One of the voices, deep and rough, sounded clearly through the night air as they approached.

"I tell you, Ed, tonight's the last job I do."

"Got the wind up then?" asked another voice.

"I just don't like it, that's all," was the reply. "We've delivered the stuff to that shelter too often for my liking."

"It's safe enough," said the other voice. "That golf course is as good a place as any."

At that moment two figures, silhouetted against the dimly moonlit sky, could be seen passing the entrance of the cave. One was tall and heavily built, the other smaller. Sue clung to Neil in the darkness, looking anxiously at the two men, hardly daring to breathe. The smaller man was carrying something heavy; it seemed to be a box or case of some kind. To Sue's horror, the man put the box down just at the mouth of the cave.

"Your turn, Phil. It's damn heavy tonight. Damn heavy."

The other man, who seemed to be older, bent down and picked up the box with a sigh.

"I wish the blasted stuff was at the bottom of the sea!" Grumbling to himself, he followed his companion up the path. The voices quickly faded into silence.

"They're smugglers all right," said Dave. "I'd like to know what they've got inside that box."

"Let's follow them up the cliff," Neil suggested suddenly. "See where they go."

"Oh no!" said Sue. "Oh, I couldn't!"

"All right, then Dave and I will go alone," Neil said quickly, too excited to consider what Sue's feelings might be. "We can't just sit here and let them get away."

Sue said nothing. The thought of being left by herself in the lonely cave frightened her, but she didn't like to say so. To her relief, Dave interrupted.

"Now look, Neil, we've got to be sensible about this. We can't leave Sue here alone. And anyway, you don't know the

way up the cliff. If you slipped up there in the dark, we'd be in a mess. You know that."

"But —"

"I tell you what we'll do. I'll go up there by myself. I know the path. And I've a good idea where that shelter is that they were talking about."

"Oh yes!" said Sue. "It must be that hut near the cliff top where people on the golf course shelter when it rains."

"That's it," said Dave. "At least, that's probably the one they meant. I'll go there and see what they're up to."

He got up, found his torch, put on a light jacket, and looked at Neil and Sue seriously.

"I'll be back in about an hour, I expect." He shone the torch onto his watch. "Good heavens! It's about twenty to one already. Right, see you later."

Before Neil had time to stop him, he had walked out of the cave, and the two friends were left in darkness.

"Be careful!" Sue called after him, but there was no reply. Dave was already on his way up the path.

6 The Boat

It seemed quieter than ever in the cave, now that Dave was no longer there. All the clouds had gone, and the moon, now high in the sky, cast a silvery light over the sea; as they looked out onto the bay, they could clearly see the black line of the cliffs on each side of them and, further away, the tops of the rocks over which they had come.

"I wish there was something we could do," said Neil at last, after they had sat in silence for a few minutes.

"We can only wait till Dave comes back. I don't expect he'll be long." Sue yawned.

"You're tired, Sue. Why don't you lie down on the air-bed and try to sleep for a while?"

"Yes, I think I will. You don't mind, do you, Neil?"

"Of course not. I don't think I could sleep anyway, I'm too excited."

Sue was soon asleep. Neil sat alone at the mouth of the cave and looked out, thinking about Dave and wishing that he had gone with him. He didn't know what Dave really intended to do when he had followed the two men to the shelter. Would he go to the police before he returned to the cave? Would he see what the contents of the heavy box were? Would he see the person whom the two men had arranged to meet, the person, Neil imagined, who had signalled from the cliff top? Or would they simply leave the box in the shelter without waiting for anyone to collect it? It was no use; Neil could not possibly guess what might now be going on up there on the golf course. He wished he was there.

The moon rose still higher in the sky, and its light became brighter. Neil looked at his watch, which he had re-set by Dave's. He was surprised to see that it was already well after half past one. Dave had been gone for nearly an hour. He ought to be back any time now.

But nothing happened. Nobody came. The tide, now half-way out, was uncovering more and more of the sand. The waves, lapping quietly onto the beach, made the only sound. At last Neil decided to wake Sue. He was beginning to wonder if anything had happened to Dave.

"Look, Sue, it's nearly two o'clock now, and Dave still isn't here. I'm getting worried about him."

Sue got up from the air-bed and went with Neil to the mouth of the cave.

"Perhaps we ought to do something, Sue."

"But what? We can't climb up the path, it's too dangerous."

"We might be able to get over those rocks now. The tide's low enough, I expect. Let's try, Sue. Then at least we won't feel so helpless as we do now. It's awful just waiting here and doing nothing."

So they left the cave and started to climb back down the path to the beach. They would have liked to leave a note, so that Dave would know where they had gone if he came back to the cave, but they couldn't find anything to write with. They soon found that the walk down to the beach was not so difficult as it had seemed on the way up; the moon gave them enough light to see the outlines of the path quite clearly. At the bottom, Neil jumped down the last few feet onto the sand and held up his hands to help Sue. At last they both stood together on the beach.

"Now for the rocks," said Neil.

They walked down to where the sea lapped onto the end of the cliff. The moon cast a pale light on the black rocks, which were still partly covered in water. The sea looked dark and forbidding, Sue thought. Neil looked at her doubtfully.

"Well, do you think we'll make it?"

"I think it's still too early to try it, Neil. Let's wait till the tide goes out a bit further."

"But the longer we wait, the worse it may be for Dave. We don't know, but something awful may have happened." Neil felt impatient.

Looking up the beach towards the cliff they had just climbed down, Sue saw the dark shape of the rowing boat, pulled up high on the sand. She suddenly had an idea.

"What about that boat? We could use that, couldn't we? We could get round the rocks in it!"

Neil hugged her excitedly. "Why didn't we think of that before? It's the best thing we could possibly do, Sue. And then, if those men come back, they won't be able to get away!"

They ran up the beach again to the boat, and began to pull it over the sand. It was old and heavy, but the two of them were able to move it without too much difficulty. Soon they had it in the water. Sue climbed inside, and Neil stood in the waves to
5 push it off. At last it was afloat, and Neil jumped up and climbed over the side. He took the oars and began to row out away from the shore.

Sue looked towards the cliff as they moved further out to sea.

"Neil! There's a light coming down the cliff! It must be those
10 two men."

"You're sure it's not Dave? He might have seen us."

Neil stopped rowing for a moment. Then, quite clearly, they both heard the sound of distant voices. The men were already at the bottom of the cliff.

15 "Quick!" cried Sue, suddenly afraid. "They'll find their boat's gone in a moment, and they're sure to see us! Oh, come on, Neil! We must get away from here."

As soon as she had spoken, they heard shouts from the top of the beach. In the pale moonlight they saw that the two men were

running down the beach towards the sea. Neil began rowing strongly out to sea. They still had to row a little further before they could safely get past the end of the rocks.

"Okay," said Neil at last. "We can pass the rocks now."

Sue's heart was beating fast. The two men had reached the sea and were shouting at them, shaking their fists. It was impossible to hear what they were saying, but it was obvious enough that they were hoping to cut them off by crossing the rocks near the cliff. It was just light enough to see two dark figures wading through the deep water at the end of the cliff.

But the boat was making good progress. The current was in their favour, and they glided smoothly over the water.

"We'll land a bit further along the beach," said Neil as they rowed past the last of the rocks into Puffin Bay itself. "It'll be some time before those two get across, if they manage it at all."

The two men were no longer in sight. Neil rowed towards the beach, now finding it difficult to fight the tide. When they were in shallow water, Neil told Sue to jump out of the boat.

"We'll wade to the beach from here!" he cried. "The boat will drift out on the tide. Come on!"

With water up to their waists, they gave the empty boat a push, and as they waded ashore, it began to drift slowly out into the open sea.

7 The Shelter

When they reached the beach, they looked back in the direction of the rocks. There was no sign yet of the two men, who were presumably still fighting their way across them, or waiting until the tide had gone out further.

"Let's go on then," said Sue. "We don't want to be in sight when they appear round the corner of the cliff."

They ran along the sand together. How different everything looked now from when they had walked along here in the opposite direction the afternoon before! Then it had been warm and sunny, now the sand was dark, the air cool, and there was only the dim light of the moon on the sea. After they had run for a few minutes, hand in hand, they turned round, but it was too dark to see whether the two men had appeared round the end of the cliff. They went on, and Neil put his arm round Sue's shoulders.

"There's no need to worry, Sue. They won't see us now."

She smiled up at him in the moonlight.

"It was a good idea to let the boat drift out to sea like that," she said. "By the time they get round those rocks, it will be far away."

"They may spend some time looking for it on the beach," said Neil. "It's still quite dark, and they won't be able to see that we didn't pull it up onto the beach! Or, of course, they may think we're still in it!"

By now they were about half-way along the Puffin Bay beach. Suddenly Neil stopped and pointed to the cliffs.

"There's a path up to the golf course here. That'll be the quickest way into the town. And we'll pass that shelter on the way."

"The path's not dangerous, is it?" asked Sue anxiously.

"Oh no, it's a public footpath down to the beach. You needn't worry."

Neil was right. The cliff path here was very different from the narrow path leading up to the cave. There were even steps in places, and a hand-rail, and in a few minutes they had reached the top. There they found themselves only a short way from the golf course. They climbed over a fence and walked over the heather until they came to the short, thick grass of the course itself.

"I think that shelter is somewhere among that group of bushes and trees over there. Do you see?"

Sue pointed to a dark, tangled shape on the moonlit horizon.

"Yes, I think you're right, Sue."

In a few minutes they reached the little group of bushes. A narrow path led from the grass on which they had been walking, through the heather, to the shelter. A light wind rustled in the bushes, and Sue clung to Neil's arm. There was something frightening about the place. Suddenly there was a noise of some movement in the bushes on their right, and Sue stopped.

"What was that?" she whispered.

"Only a bird or a mouse, I expect," Neil answered. "Come on."

They walked further along the little path, turned a corner, and there, with bushes on each side of it, stood the shelter. The door was open.

"Shall we go in?" Sue whispered, still rather afraid.

"Of course."

They walked up to the door. Just as they were approaching it, Neil stepped on something hard. He stopped and bent down to see what it was.

"Dave's torch! So he must have been here all right!"

He switched the torch on. The bright yellow light made the shadows around them deeper and blacker, the night quieter and more mysterious. Sue held Neil's arm more tightly, and they entered the shelter. It was a small hut, built of wood, and there was a smell of damp grass inside it. Wooden benches ran along the walls for the sheltering golfers to sit on.

Neil flashed the torch round the inside of the hut. They both suddenly gasped. In one of the corners, with his back turned to the door, they saw Dave lying in a heap on the floor.

"Dave! Oh no! How awful!" cried Sue, standing in the middle of the hut, her eyes full of fear.

Neil ran across to where Dave was lying, and bent over him. "Dave! Dave, are you hurt?"

He touched Dave's arm, then shook his shoulder. Dave moved slightly at his touch, and groaned.

"Wake up, Dave!"

Dave turned his face, and Neil shone the torch down onto it. On the top of Dave's forehead, just below the line of untidy hair, Neil saw a large bruise, dark and inflamed, and a smear of dried blood.

The light of the torch made Dave open his eyes for a moment, but he did not seem to have recognized Neil, and turned his face back to the wall.

"He's been hit on the head, Sue. It looks pretty serious. We must get help at once. He must have been lying here for well over two hours already."

"But we can't leave him here alone!" said Sue.

"Well, one of us must phone for an ambulance," Neil answered. "He'll have to be taken to hospital. I'll go and phone, and you can stay here with him."

Sue looked worried.

"Oh, I couldn't, Neil! Here in this lonely place? Oh please don't leave me! Imagine if those men came back!"

"Well then, Dave will have to be left alone till the ambulance arrives, unless you want to leave me here with him."

Sue shook her head.

"We'll go to the telephone-box together," she said. "Come on!"

So together they ran out of the shelter, along the path through the heather, and down towards the town.

8 Two Pretty Fish

By the time they reached the telephone-box on Cliff Avenue, Neil and Sue were quite out of breath from running. It had taken them about ten minutes to get there from the golf course, and when Neil looked at his watch as they stopped outside the box for a moment to get their breath back, he was surprised to see that it was already well after four. They went into the telephone-box together, and Neil picked up the receiver, dialled 999 and asked for the police.

A police officer answered the phone, and Neil quickly told him about their adventures. How they had been cut off by the tide and forced to wait in the cave in the little bay, and how they had seen the signals and later the two men with their mysterious box. How they had made use of the men's boat to get away, and finally how they had found Dave in the shelter on the golf course.

"The most important thing's an ambulance," he said. "Dave looks as if he's been badly hurt."

A moment later he put the receiver down and turned to Sue.

"A police car's coming to pick us up here in a few minutes," he said. "And do you know what the policeman said? They've been out looking for us all over the town!"

"Oh, I knew our parents would be worried when we didn't come in. They must have felt awful! Oh dear, what a lot of trouble we've been causing."

They didn't have long to wait before a large, black police car drew up at the kerb, and a tall, rather fat sergeant got out.

"Hello, young man," he said to Neil at once. "Are you Neil McLaren? And is this your friend Susan? You just jump in the car with us."

He opened the back door of the police car, and Neil and Sue got in. Climbing into the front seat himself, next to the driver, a younger policeman with short dark hair, he turned round to talk to them. The car moved off.

"We're driving down to the sea-front now. There's still a chance those two men may be down on the beach. Let me see now — how long ago was it that you left them making their way round the rocks at the end of the beach?"

Neil thought for a moment. "By the time we got to Puffin Bay beach, it must have been between half past two and three o'clock. About an hour and a half or two hours ago, then."

"Do our parents know we're all right?" asked Sue, who didn't like to think of her mother worrying about her.

"Oh yes, they know you're safe," the sergeant reassured her.

"And what about the ambulance?" Sue went on anxiously. "Will they be able to drive it up to the shelter all right?"

"No problem at all," said the sergeant. "There's a rough road leading up there. The groundsmen on the golf course need it for moving about the course with their equipment, you know." He turned to the policeman on his right. "We'll stop somewhere near the 'Smuggler's Arms', Parker."

As they looked out of the car window, they saw that it was getting much lighter. Sunrise could not be far away now. A few moments later they stopped on the sea-front, not far from the 'Smuggler's Arms'.

The two policemen got out of the car, and Neil and Sue followed. The first grey light of morning had appeared in the sky, and the sea, which had looked so mysterious and unfriendly in the moonlight, was beginning to take on its familiar daytime colours again. Several fishermen were preparing their boats and pulling them down the beach, others were already out on the sea. This part of the beach, reserved for the fishermen, was covered with boats of all sizes, with nets and with lobster-pots.

They looked along the beach in the direction of the rocks, but there was nobody to be seen.

"It looks as if they've gone," said Sue.

"Would you recognize them again if you saw them?" asked Constable Parker.

"I think so," said Neil, "though of course it was dark when they passed the cave, and we couldn't see their faces very clearly."

"But we should certainly recognize their voices!" said Sue.

Suddenly Neil pointed to a shining, expensive-looking motor-boat at the edge of the water, which contrasted strongly with the simple boats used by the fishermen.

"What's that?" he said, surprised. "It's not one of yours, is it, Sergeant?"

A broad smile appeared on the sergeant's chubby, red face. "We arranged for it to be ready at day-break, so that we could go and search for you two if necessary — that was before we got your phone-call, of course. But now we may be able to make rather different use of it."

Neil looked puzzled.

"It's possible that those two men have got away by now in one of the fishing boats," the sergeant explained.

Neil looked at the tiny boats far out in the bay.

"So we'll go out in our little speed-boat and have a look! Coming with us, son?" The sergeant looked at Sue. "As for you, Susan, you'd better go along back to your hotel for some sleep. Tell your parents all about your adventures."

"All right," said Sue, and turned to go. "I don't suppose I can be much help. See you later, Neil. And good luck!"

The sergeant got into the motor-boat, and Neil and Constable Parker followed. A moment later they were moving out to sea, and Sue, looking back, saw the boat speeding further and further away into the distance.

Neil had never been out in a motor-boat like this one before. It cut through the water like a sharp knife, and in no time they had left the beach far behind them and were approaching the small fishing boats now scattered all over the bay. As they went past the first boats, a few of the brown-faced, friendly fishermen nodded to them and smiled. There was no sign so far of the two men they were looking for. But still further out on the waves more boats were to be seen. On they went through the deep green water, on which the first low rays of sunshine were falling, until Neil pointed ahead in excitement.

"Those could be the men! Out there in that boat all by itself — I'm almost sure!"

As they came nearer, Neil became more and more certain that he was right. A small fishing boat with an outboard motor was slowly moving further out into the bay; in it sat two men.

"They seem to be making for that yacht out there!" said Constable Parker, who was now steering the motor-boat towards the smaller boat with the two men on board. "The yacht's waiting out there to pick them up, I bet!"

Sure enough, a large yacht could be seen still further out on the waves, and the small fishing boat was making its way towards it. The sound of the approaching motor-boat made one of the men turn round.

"They've seen us!" cried Neil.

At that moment the smaller of the two men, who had looked back and seen the policemen's blue uniforms, took out a gun, aimed, and fired.

"Get down, Neil! Lie flat on your stomach — they're firing!" the sergeant cried out. "Go for them, Parker!"

As Neil lay down, he felt the motor-boat surge forward with new power. Three more shots were fired. Looking up over the side of the boat for a second, Neil saw that they were now only a few yards away from the small fishing boat, which had not the speed to compete with the large police boat. They were making straight for it now. It looked as if there would be a collision.

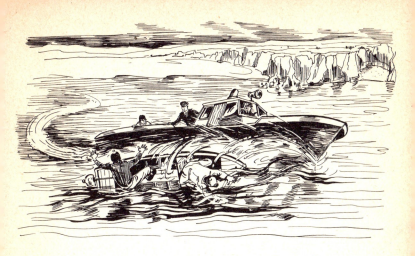

Nearer and nearer they came. Neil ducked down again and waited for the crash.

Instead, the motor-boat lurched violently to the left and a sudden wave of spray splashed onto the small deck. There were
5 shouts of dismay. Neil pushed back his wet hair from his face and looked over the side.

"Well done, Parker!" the sergeant was crying out, a wide smile on his plump face. "Well done!"

Neil saw immediately what had happened. The violent move-
10 ment which they had made so close to the other boat had been too much for it. A large wave had crashed into the side of the fishing boat, which had at once capsized.

They turned round and began to move slowly back to the scene of the accident. The two men were floundering about in
15 the water, trying, without success, to turn their capsized craft over again. The large motor-boat stopped, and the sergeant leaned over the side, smiling to himself. Seeing the hopelessness of their position, the two men swore at him, but he only laughed.

"Can we offer you a free trip back to the coast?" he said, and then turned to the constable. "Pull them in, Parker."

Ropes were thrown out, and the two men, soaking wet and silent with anger, were pulled over the side. The older one, whose name, Neil remembered, was Phil, was gasping for breath, and the other looked sullenly at Neil, but said nothing.

"There'll be plenty for you two to explain when we get to the station," said the sergeant, "so you'd better start thinking hard!"

"What about the yacht?" said Neil to Constable Parker, as the motor-boat headed for the shore.

"We've no chance of catching her," Constable Parker replied. He turned and pointed to the yacht, which was now hardly more than a dot on the horizon. "As soon as she reaches international waters, there's nothing we can do."

"But we've caught two pretty fish this morning already," said the sergeant, looking at the two men. "This is a big organization, I expect. We can't hope to wipe it out in one day, Neil. But we've made a start."

9 The 'Major'

It was half past seven, and the bright morning sun shone in through the open window of the small hospital room. In the high hospital bed, a large white bandage round his head, Dave was sitting, a cup of tea in his hand. He had been awake now for an hour, and although his head still ached a little, he was feeling much better. The injury had not been serious after all, but he was to stay in hospital for the rest of the day, nevertheless.

There was a knock at the door, and a nurse came in. The sergeant and Neil followed.

"Try not to excite him too much, please," said the nurse with a friendly smile. "What he needs most at the moment is rest, you know."

She went out and left them together. Neil ran forward.

"Dave! Are you all right?"

"I've got a bit of a headache, that's all! But I must say it was quite a surprise to wake up and find myself here in a hospital bed!"

"Right then, Mr —" the sergeant began.

"Wainwright," said Dave. "David Wainwright."

"I'd be very pleased if you'd tell me just what happened to you at that shelter on the golf course last night."

"We've caught those two men!" Neil interrupted. "They were..."

"We'll tell him our story later, Neil," said the sergeant. "Let Mr Wainwright tell us what happened to him first."

Slowly and carefully, not wanting to forget any important details, Dave told his story. With his torch in his hand, he had climbed up the cliff path after the two men, and had made his way across the golf course to the group of bushes where he knew the shelter was.

"I soon found the little path that leads up to the shelter," Dave said. "It was pretty dark along there, with trees and bushes all round, but I switched my torch off. I didn't want to be seen. And then, just as I came to a corner of the path and saw the dark shape of the shelter in front of me, I heard the sound of voices. So someone was still there! I went a bit nearer, very quietly of course, stood outside the shelter and listened. Then I recognized the voices. They were the same ones as we'd heard on the cliff path. The two men I'd followed were still there. I decided I might get to know more if I waited outside the shelter and listened to what they were saying.

"Then I heard a third voice, one which I didn't recognize. It was obviously the voice of the man they had arranged to meet — the one who had signalled from the cliff top. He sounded better educated than the other two, and I realized from what was being said that he was their boss."

"What exactly did you overhear then?" asked the sergeant, leaning over the bed with interest. "What did they say?"

"They were speaking in rather low voices," Dave went on, "so I didn't understand everything, but from what I was able to hear, it seemed that the two who had brought the goods up the cliff were dissatisfied and asking for more money. You remember the one called Phil, who had said before that he didn't want to do any more of these jobs?" he asked Neil.

Neil nodded.

"Well, he was doing most of the talking. But the man who seemed to be their boss — 'Major', that's what they both called him — he said they were being given enough, and wouldn't get a penny more."

"Did you see this man at all? The Major, I mean?" asked the sergeant.

"Yes, I did. He came out of the shelter soon after I arrived, and left the other two still talking together."

"Could you describe him?"

"Oh no, it was too dark to see him properly. He was fairly tall, I think, but even on that point I can't be really sure — he was rather bent with carrying that box, you see. Rather vague, I'm afraid."

"Did any of them say anything about what sort of goods they were actually smuggling?" asked the sergeant.

"No, they didn't," Dave replied. "I kept hoping that they would. But they just talked about the 'stuff' all the time — nothing more definite than that.

"In the end, after the man called the Major had gone, I made up my mind to go and telephone the police. But just at that moment the other two emerged from the shelter and caught sight of me. It all happened quickly after that. Before I had time to realize what was going on, one of them had knocked the torch out of my hand and the other had grabbed my shoulders. Then I must have been hit on the head and put in the shelter, but I don't remember that part of it."

"It was lucky they didn't shoot," said Neil. "One of them had a gun, you know. The small one called Ed."

"Right," said the sergeant, getting up to go. "We'll leave you to have a good rest, Mr Wainwright. Many thanks for the information you've just given me."

"I hope you find the Major, Sergeant," said Dave. "Any idea who he might be?"

"Not yet, I'm afraid." The sergeant looked at Neil. "Come on, son, you need some rest too."

"Yes, I'll be pleased to get back to the hotel," said Neil. He had an idea. "Why don't you join us and our parents for dinner tonight, Dave? You're allowed to leave here this evening, aren't you?"

"Thanks, Neil, that would be fine. What's the name of your hotel?"

"The 'Smuggler's Arms'. Appropriate, isn't it?"

10 At the Dinner Table

"If I'd been you," said Jimmy, turning to Sue as they sat at the dinner table that evening, "I certainly would have followed those two men up the cliff path. Wouldn't you, Bruce?"

"You bet. I wouldn't have let them get away so easily," said Bruce, his mouth full of ice-cream.

"What would you have done then, young man?" They all turned round. They had been so deep in their conversation that they hadn't noticed Mr Wallace approaching their table.

"Goodness, Mr Wallace, you gave us all quite a shock," said Mrs McLaren, turning round to the manager, who stood one or two feet in front of them, tall and dark, his moustache a black stroke above his mouth.

"I'm awfully sorry," Mr Wallace smiled. "I didn't intend to steal up on you, but you were talking so excitedly that you didn't hear me. How are our two fugitives then? I only heard about your adventures this morning."

"Yes, we were all rather worried last night, Mr Wallace," said Mr Johnson. "We thought something might have happened to Susan and Neil. When it was past midnight and they still weren't back, we rang the police. We tried of find you first, but your wife couldn't tell us where you were."

"What a pity, Mr Johnson! I always stay with a friend on Friday nights, I'm afraid. But the main thing is our two heroes are back safe and sound. Jolly good show. Excellent, excellent!"

"Will you please excuse me a moment?" Dave had been desperately busy with his cheese and biscuits ever since Mr Wallace had come to their table. Now he clumsily left the table, apparently choking on a piece of Danish Blue and awkwardly bumping into Neil as he got up.

"Poor Dave," said Mrs McLaren, "I hope he's all right after that nasty affair. Go on, Neil, go and see."

While Neil left the table Mr Wallace was asked to sit down, and Mr Johnson started to explain Dave's role in the previous night's adventures.

"Yes, we ought to have introduced our new friend, Mr Wainwright," he said. "He's the young biologist who was camping out in the cave. Spending his holidays doing a bit of research, I believe."

"Oh really?" said Mr Wallace. "He looked as if he'd been in a bit of a fight, I noticed. However did he get that nasty bruise?"

"Didn't you know?" said Sue. "It was those two men. At the shelter on the golf course. He'd been listening to their conversation, you see."

"What's the matter, Mr Wallace?" asked Bruce, who had been quietly sitting there, studying the manager's face, for the last few moments.

Everyone looked at Mr Wallace, who laughed stiffly.

"I'm afraid my thoughts were elsewhere," he explained with a wave of the hand. "The new chambermaid, you know. My wife's been having a bit of trouble with her. I –" he hesitated. "Yes, well I'm sure you don't want to hear all the details."

"Tell us again about what happened when you and Neil got to the shelter, Sue!" said Jimmy eagerly. "You haven't heard about it, have you, Mr Wallace?"

"Pardon? Sorry, yes of course, I'm most interested."

Sue told her story, and in the soft light of the hotel dining-room the terrors of the previous night seemed to be almost forgotten, and Sue had returned to her old, confident self. Mr Wallace listened, playing with a long, unlit cigar which he held between his fingers. All the others knew the story, but they were enjoying hearing it again from Sue's angle.

"Those two are taking rather a long time," said Mrs Johnson, when Sue had got to the bit about Neil and the sergeant visiting Dave in hospital. "Do go and have a look what's going on out there, Jimmy."

Jimmy left the table, skipping through the dining-room.

"And do you know who the police are looking for now, Mr. Wallace?" Bruce interrupted.

"No, I've no idea. Have they got any clues?"

"Yes, of course! They're looking for a Major or a Colonel!" Bruce burst out. "Because Dave overheard those two talking to him. It's very easy now – they just have to check up on the former army officers around here, and then — bang!"

39

Mr McLaren laughed and turned to Mr Wallace, who was staring at Bruce. "Well done, Sherlock Holmes!" he said. "What he means, Mr Wallace, is this —"

"They've both gone! They're not in Neil's bedroom, and they're not in the loo either!" Jimmy shouted across the dining-room.

"Jimmy!" Mrs Johnson cried, and the guests at the other tables turned round and smiled.

Mr Wallace had half risen from his chair. He bowed stiffly to the ladies.

"I'm sorry to interrupt your story, Mr McLaren," he said, "but I really ought to go and help my wife with the accounts now."

He bowed again stiffly, turned round and left the room, his head held erect, his steps quick and decisive.

11 The Smuggler's Arms

"That was a jolly good bit of acting you did in that dining-room, Dave," Neil said, turning to Dave who was sitting behind him.

"Acting? I almost choked when I recognized the voice. It gave me the shock of my life!"

"I only hope you're not mistaken. But I must say, our information from London may very well confirm your suspicions." Sergeant Miller, who was driving the police car himself this time, looked at Dave in the mirror. There were two more policemen in the back of the big car, one of whom was Constable Parker.

"I shouldn't be surprised if Wrigley and Sharp decide to co-operate," said Constable Parker. "I mean the two men we caught this morning," he explained when he saw Dave's questioning look.

"You think they'll identify him as the Major then?" Neil asked.

"I expect so," answered Constable Parker. "They'll turn King's evidence, I feel sure."

"King's evidence?" said Neil. "What's that?"

Sergeant Miller explained. "When you give incriminating evidence against an accomplice, we call it King's evidence. Some criminals give their friends away like that, hoping that they won't be punished so severely when the case goes to court. Those two may even give us some useful information about the rest of the gang — you never know."

Neil nodded. "I see. Well, let's hope so."

The car turned the last corner and then went down the seafront, approaching the 'Smuggler's Arms'. When they were a few yards away from the hotel, they saw a car coming out of the drive.

"Park in front of the gates, Sarge!" said the third policeman.

"Good idea, Wills," said Sergeant Miller, stopping the police car at the entrance to the hotel drive.

The reversing car, unable to go any further, was forced to stop, and Mr Wallace got out, his face white and his dark eyes flashing.

"Don't you realize there's no parking outside my gates?" he stormed. "You're blocking the entrance to my hotel. I —"

Mr Wallace stopped in surprise. Three policemen had stepped out of the big black car in front of him.

"We'd like to have a look at your car, if you don't mind, sir," said the sergeant, quietly but firmly.

"I don't see what right you have," Mr Wallace began to protest.

Constable Parker produced a search warrant, and the ex-

pression on the hotel proprietor's face suddenly changed from one of anger to one of fear. Reluctantly he handed over the key.

Constable Wills took it and at once opened up the boot of the car. They all looked inside and saw a large wooden case.

5 "Is this it?" Sergeant Miller said to Neil.

"It looks very much like it."

"Open it, Parker, please," Sergeant Miller said, and a moment later the lid of the case was removed and the contents uncovered. Dozens of small slabs, wrapped in silver paper, were packed next 10 to each other in neat rows. The sergeant picked one up and opened it. Inside the silver paper was a dark brown mass of something which looked a little like tightly pressed tobacco. He lifted it to his nose and smelt it.

"Yes, it's hashish all right. Thirty or forty pounds of it! Like 15 to smell it, son?" he asked Neil.

Neil did so. "Just like the smell of hay!" he exclaimed in surprise. "But it looks rather like a bar of chocolate, doesn't it?"

"Just a little bit more expensive than chocolate, though!" said Constable Wills. "Four or five hundred times as much, I shouldn't wonder."

"Well, Mr Wallace," said the sergeant, and everyone looked at the proprietor of the 'Smuggler's Arms', whose face was drawn and very pale, "I think you'd better come along with us to the station now."

Coffee was being served in the hotel lounge. None of the other guests seemed to have missed Mr Wallace.

"Yes, it was terrible when I recognized that voice!" said Dave, laughing now as he remembered how he had behaved at the dinner table. "As soon as he came over to the table, I knew the voice was familiar. And then when he said 'Jolly good show' and 'Excellent, excellent', I knew at once who it was!"

"I always thought that was funny!" interrupted Jimmy eagerly. "Jolly good show! Excellent, excellent!" he mimicked, and everyone roared with laughter. "He always said that when Dad told him the dinner was good."

"And did he really say the same to those two men at the shelter? — What were their names?" said Sue.

"Wrigley and Sharp," Neil remembered.

"Yes, it's funny, isn't it?" Dave looked at them all with a grin. "He'd been trying to persuade those two to go on working for him and his gang. They agreed in the end, and that's when he said 'Jolly good show'. Not many people use the expression, and I remembered it, of course."

"It's just as well we're all going home tomorrow," said Mr McLaren. "The hotel will be at sixes and sevens for a while after all this! Poor Mrs Wallace."

"What an appropriate name they had for him!" said Mrs McLaren. "He really looked just like an army officer with that little moustache — and the way he walked!"

"Let's hope the police catch up with the rest of the gang," Mr Johnson said. "A nasty affair, smuggling drugs. I wonder who old Wallace sold the stuff to... Well, it'll all be in the papers soon enough, I suppose."

"Yes," said Bruce, "and there are sure to be pictures of Sue and Neil in the papers too! They might even be shown on T.V.!"

"Gosh, Sue!" teased Jimmy. "You'd better go upstairs and comb your hair — the cameramen might be here any moment!"

"Well, there's one thing certain about all this," said Dave. "It'll be a marvellous advertisement for the hotel here. The next owner will have good reason to spin a few yarns about the 'Smuggler's Arms'!"

Questions about the Story

1 Holidays at Puffin Bay

a) What sort of a hotel was the 'Smuggler's Arms'?
b) Who were the McTaggarts?
c) What kind of a person was Mr Wallace?
d) Why were his guests so happy?
e) Why had the Johnson family come to the 'Smuggler's Arms'?
f) How old were the McLarens' two sons?
g) When had Neil first seen Sue?
h) How did the two families spend their time in Cornwall?
i) What did plans they make one evening?

2 On the Beach

a) What did the three boys do before breakfast?
b) Why didn't Sue go into the water with Neil after breakfast?
c) What did Neil do after he came out of the water?
d) What did Sue and Neil decide to do after their swim?
e) Why did Sue look doubtful when Neil suggested walking round the end of the cliff?
f) What did they see when they came round the end of the cliff?

3 Surprised by the Tide

a) Why didn't many people go to the little bays between Puffin Bay and Starmouth?
b) Why did Sue and Neil stay so late?
c) What had happened to the rocks?

d) What did they try to do first, and why didn't they succeed?
e) What was Neil worried about?
f) What was the only way of escape?
g) What did the cliffs look like?
h) Why was Sue frightened when they climbed up the cliff path?

4   The Cave

a) Why did they decide to stay in the cave?
b) Why wasn't it possible to see the cave from the beach?
c) What did they suddenly hear?
d) Who was the stranger and why was he living in the cave?
e) How did the three of them spend the evening?
f) Where did they see lights?

5   Figures in the Dark

a) What did they see and hear from the cave?
b) Why did they move to the back of the cave?
c) What did the two men say as they went past the cave?
d) What did Neil want to do when they had gone?
e) Why didn't Dave agree with his suggestion, and what did he decide to do himself?

6   The Boat

a) What did Sue and Neil do while they were waiting for Dave to come back?
b) Why did Neil begin to worry, and what did he do then?
c) Why didn't he and Sue go across the rocks?
d) What did they decide to do?
e) What happened when the two men came down the cliff?
f) Why did Sue and Neil let the boat drift out to sea?

7 The Shelter

a) What was the difference between the Puffin Bay cliff path and the other cliff path?
b) What did the shelter on the golf course look like in the moonlight?
c) How did Neil know that Dave had been there?
d) What did they see in one of the corners?
e) What had happened to Dave?
f) What did they decide to do next?

8 Two Pretty Fish

a) What did Neil tell the police officer over the telephone?
b) What did the police officer tell him?
c) Why did they drive down to the sea-front in the police car?
d) What did they see on the beach and in the bay?
e) Why was the expensive-looking motor-boat there, and what was it used for now?
f) Why didn't Sue go out in the boat with the others?
g) What sort of a boat were the two men they were looking for in?
h) What happened when the two men saw the motor-boat?
i) How did the police catch the men?
j) Why didn't they go after the yacht?

9 The 'Major'

a) Who came to see Dave in hospital?
b) How many voices had he heard in the shelter?
c) What was the subject of the men's conversation?
d) What did Dave decide to do after the 'Major' had gone?
e) What happened then?
f) What did Neil suggest before he and the sergeant left?

10 At the Dinner Table

a) Why did Mr Wallace give the two families a shock when he came up at dinner?
b) Why did Mrs McLaren ask Neil to leave the room?
c) Why did Jimmy leave the table, and what news did he bring when he came back?
d) What reason did Mr Wallace give for leaving the room?

11 The Smuggler's Arms

a) Whose voice did Dave recognize in the dining-room?
b) Who were Wrigley and Sharp?
c) How did Sergeant Miller explain 'King's evidence'?
d) Why did Constable Wills suggest parking in front of the hotel gates?
e) What made Mr Wallace's expression change so suddenly?
f) What was inside the boot of Mr Wallace's car?
g) How did Sergeant Miller know what the brown mass was?
h) How had Mr Wallace given himself away at the dinner table?
i) Why did Wrigley and Sharp call their boss 'Major'?
j) How did Dave think that the affair would affect the hotel?

Compositions

a) *A Day on the Beach*
   Describe a day you have spent at the seaside, or what people usually do when they are on the beach.

b) *Staying at a Hotel*
   What is life like at a hotel? Describe what happens when guests come and go, at meal times, in the evenings, and so on.

c) *Smugglers at Puffin Bay* (A Newspaper Report)
   Write an informative article about the smugglers and how they were discovered and caught.

d) *At the Police Station*
   Try to imagine what happened to Wrigley and Sharp and to Mr Wallace when they were questioned at the police station. What were they asked, and what were their answers?

e) *Constable Parker Talks to his Wife*
   and tells her how he helped to catch three members of a gang of smugglers.

f) *A Letter from Sue or Neil*
   Imagine that you are Sue or Neil, and write a letter to a schoolfriend, telling her/him all about your adventures.

g) *Smuggling Drugs*
   Try to imagine how the gang in this story worked, where and how they got the drugs and what they did with them. How do you think the police would try to catch the rest of the gang?

Test your Grammar

How good is your English grammar? Test your knowledge by doing these exercises; the page numbers refer to the pages in this book where the sentences appear, so you can easily check and correct your work yourself.

Past Tense or Present Perfect?

a) It must have been low tide when we (to come) over the rocks this afternoon at three. *p. 13/14*
b) I (to be) here about a week now. *p. 15*
c) We (to be only) here a few minutes, and when we (to come) it (to be) too dark to see anything much in here. *p. 15/16*
d) How long ago (to be) it that you (to leave) them making their way round the rocks? *p. 30*
e) Then I (to hear) a third voice, one which I (not to recognize). *p. 35*
f) Many thanks for the information you (just to give) me. *p. 37*
g) When they (to be) a few yards away from the hotel, they (to see) a car. *p. 41*

Past Tense — Ordinary or Continuous?

a) Mr Wallace (to look) as if a military uniform would suit him better than the casual clothes he always (to wear). *p. 4*
b) When she (to get) to the beach, he (to stand) on the sand. *p. 8*
c) As they (to look) out of the car window, they (to see) that it (to get) much lighter. *p. 30*

d) There (to be) no sign so far of the two men they (to look for). *p. 32*
e) I (not to intend to) steal up on you, but you (to talk) so excitedly that you (not to hear) me. *p. 38*
f) Sergeant Miller, who (to drive) the police car himself this time, (to look) at Dave in the mirror. *p. 40*

If and *When* Clauses

a) If he had been alone, he (may do) it. *p. 10*
b) Heaven knows what our parents (to think) when we don't come back this evening. *p. 14*
c) If you fell off the path, you (to be) lucky to escape with a broken leg. No, I'd go back the way you came if I (to be) you. *p. 16*
d) Would you recognize them again if you (to see) them? *p. 31*
e) There'll be plenty for you two to explain when we (to get) to the station. *p. 34*
f) If I'd been you, I certainly (to follow) those two men. *p. 37*

Active and Passive

1. *Turn into Passive* (Use *by* where shown!):
a) For some years a jovial Scotsman called Mr McTaggart had owned the 'Smuggler's Arms' (by). *p. 3*
b) Neil quickly told him about their adventures. How the tide had cut them off (by). *p. 29*
c) They could see a large yacht still further out on the waves. *p. 32*
d) They were serving coffee in the hotel lounge. *p. 43*

2. *Turn into Active:*
a) The moon was covered by clouds again for a few minutes. *p. 18*

b) The shadows around them were made deeper and blacker by the bright yellow light. *p. 27*
c) Your suspicions may very well be confirmed by our information from London. *p. 40*
d) The expression is not used by many people. *p. 43*

Infinitive or Gerund?

a) What about (to wait) in here until the tide goes out? *p. 13*
b) Or would they simply leave the box in the shelter without (to wait) for anyone (to collect) it? *p. 22*
c) Neil stopped (to row) for a moment. *p. 24*
d) There's no need (to worry). *p. 26*
e) We can't hope (to wipe) it out in one day. *p. 34*
f) I kept (to hope) that they would. *p. 36*
g) All the others knew the story, but they were enjoying (to hear) it again. *p. 39*

Adjective or Adverb?

a) Now it had been modernized and made very (comfortable) and (attractive). *p. 3*
b) Sue lay back (comfortable) and began to read. She felt too (lazy) for bathing yet. *p. 7*
c) The sea looked (dark) and (forbidding), Sue thought. Neil looked at her (doubtful). *p. 23*
d) The motor-boat lurched (violent) to the left and a (sudden) wave of spray splashed onto the (small) deck. *p. 33*
e) Oh no, it was too (dark) to see him (proper). *p. 36*
f) He bowed again (stiff), turned round and left the room, his head held (erect), his steps (quick) and (decisive). *p. 40*

Prepositions

a) The two families had met ... dinner ... the first evening ... their holiday. *p. 5*
b) When she got ... the beach, he was standing ... the sand, waiting ... her. *p. 8*
c) Come on, hurry ...! We'll never be back ... seven thirty ... dinner now. *p. 10*
d) Who else would come out here ... the cliff top ... this time and make signals ... a boat out ... sea? *p. 18*
e) Sue clung ... Neil ... the darkness, looking anxiously ... the two men. *p. 19*
f) The thought ... being left ... herself ... the lonely cave frightened her. *p. 20*
g) Suddenly Neil pointed ... a shining, expensive-looking motor-boat ... the edge ... the water, which contrasted strongly ... the simple boats used ... the fishermen. *p. 31*
h) Everyone roared ... laughter *p. 43*

Some or *Any* (or their compounds)?

a) All round the beach the cliffs rose steeply up from the sand, and he could not see ... place where they might escape. *p. 11*
b) Isn't that ... sort of path? *p. 11*
c) When we came it was too dark to see ... much in here. *p. 16*
d) ... is answering that signal. *p. 17*
e) If the moon comes out, we might see ... *p. 18*
f) Or would they simply leave the box in the shelter without waiting for ... to collect it? *p. 22*
g) I think that shelter is ... among that group of bushes. *p. 27*

Vocabulary

1 Holidays at Puffin Bay

3 puffin — sea-bird which is sometimes seen in the South and West of England

smuggler — person who brings things into or out of a country illegally

Arms — *here:* often the name for a hotel in England

sea-front — road in town which runs near the sea

jovial — 'dʒəuvjəl — very friendly and smiling

popular — well-liked

to persuade s.o. — pə'sweid — to try to make s.o. do what you want

efficient — i'fiʃənt — good at one's work

4 to run — to manage, to look after (a business)

customer — person who buys something

apart from — except

plump — a little fat

untidy — not very orderly

erect — standing up straight

neat — orderly, *here:* carefully cut

moustache — məs'tɑːʃ — hair on top lip

casual — 'kæʒjuəl — everyday, not special

so far — until now

slim — not fat

to catch a glimpse of — to see only for a moment

instinctively — *here:* at once, without thinking it over

cliff — high rocky piece of land (near the sea)

beach		piece of land (often sandy) at the edge of the sea
5 aged sixteen		sixteen years old
to look forward to s.th.		to think happily about s.th. in the future
tennis racket		you hit the tennis ball with it
picnic lunch		lunch to be eaten outside
to take s.o. on		to give s.o. a game
all the same		in spite of it, nevertheless
6 golf course		piece of land where people play golf
moat		water round a castle (to protect it)

2 On the Beach

sun-top		kind of blouse, to wear in hot weather
7 chef	ʃef	(male) cook in hotel or restaurant
to lap		(of sea) to come in softly, with small waves
gull	gʌl	sea-bird
swimming-trunks		man's or boy's swimsuit
to turn into		to become
to shrug one's shoulders		to raise one's shoulders (often when not knowing an answer)
bucket	'bʌkit	thing for carrying water in (often made of metal or plastic)
spade		tool used for digging
giant *(adj.)*	'dʒaiənt	very big
drawbridge		bridge over moat which can be lifted (drawn up)
youngster		young person
in no time		very quickly
to race s.o.		to try to go faster than s.o.
8 you'd better give me a start		it would be a good idea if you let me start first
to catch up with s.o.		to reach s.o. (in a race)

crawl		swimming style (fast)
breast stroke	brest	swimming style (slow)
to grin		to smile
tide		rise and fall of the sea
steep		rising sharply
to jut out	dʒʌt	to stick out
slippery		easy to slip on
seaweed		plant growing under the sea
sea anemone	ə'neməni	animal which looks like a flower growing in the sea
crab		ten-legged sea-animal with a hard shell

3 Surprised by the Tide

9 Gosh!		Good heavens!
10 waist		middle of body
ledge		*here:* flat piece of cliff
11 high tide		time at which sea is highest
half-way up		between the bottom and the top
to stare		to look hard
weeds		unwanted plants
zig-zag		in the form of a 'Z'
face		*here:* part which rises like a wall
12 to take hold of		to seize, to take in one's hand
uneven		rough, not smooth to walk on

4 The Cave

13 to slope down		to go down from high to low
It was no good trying		It was useless to try
low tide		time at which sea is lowest
14 outline		*here:* shape, form
well set back		a long way back
to elope	i'ləup	to run away together in order to get married secretly
nowadays		now, in our time
to tease	ti:z	to make s.o. angry in a playful way; *here:* to joke
to tighten		to become tight

56

rhythmically	'riðmikəli	with a steady movement
to cling to, clung, clung		to hold on tight
15 to flash		(of light) to appear for a moment
torch		*here:* battery-operated light which you can put in your pocket
mysterious	mis'tiəriəs	difficult to understand, strange
to have no business to		not to be allowed to
dim		not bright
subject		*here:* what a person studies
wild-life		wild animals, birds etc.
to turn out to be s.th.		to be found to be s.th.
harmless		not dangerous
virgin country	'və:dʒin	land where nobody has been
16 air-bed		rubber 'bed' filled with air
pretty *(adv.)*		quite
tricky		*here:* difficult
to share		to have part of
meagre	'mi:gə	*here:* simple
not up to much		not very good
camp-stove		cooking-ring used by campers
hunk	hʌnk	large piece
can		tin
however?		how?!
17 to be sheltered from the wind		to be out of the wind, protected from it
envious	'enviəs	wishing to be in another person's place
to gaze		to look for a long time
lighthouse		building with a light to help or warn ships
morse	mɔ:s	method of signalling
to make fun of		to laugh at

5 Figures in the Dark

18 what the signals were about		what the meaning of the signals was
code		key, system of signals

that's no good to us		that can't help us
goings-on		events, things that happen
to deliver	di'livə	to bring (goods) to s.o.
what they're up to		what they're doing
presumably	pri'zju:məbli	probably
to thin out		to become thinner, less thick
to cast, cast, cast		to throw
19 to make out		to recognize the shape of
oars	ɔ:z	long pieces of wood which are used to row a boat
strip		long, thin piece
uneasy		worried
in suspense	səs'pens	in a state of excitement, not knowing what will happen
(Have you) got the wind up?		(slang) Are you afraid?
shelter		*here:* small building where people go to get out of the rain, wind etc.
too often for my liking		so often that I don't like it
as good a place as any		as good as any other place
silhouetted	ˌsilu(:)'etid	seen in outline
To Sue's horror ...		Sue was frightened when ...
20 (It's) your turn		It's time for you to do something
damn	dæm	(slang) here: very
blasted	'blɑ:stid	(slang) awful
to grumble	'grʌmbl	to complain
to fade		to become weaker, to die away
to her relief ...	ri'li:f	she felt better when ...
sensible		not silly
21 to be in a mess		*here:* to be in a bad position
hut		simple building often made of wood

6 The Boat

to yawn	jɔ:n	to open one's mouth and breathe in deeply when tired
22 to arrange to meet		to plan to meet
to re-set	'ri:'set	*here:* to put right

23	Now for the rocks	Now let's go to the rocks
	forbidding	*here:* dangerous
	to make it	to succeed
	impatient	not wanting to wait
	to hug s.o.	to put one's arms round s.o.
	to get away	to escape
24	afloat ə'fləut	floating on the water
25	fist	closed hand
	obvious 'ɔbviəs	clear, easy to see or understand
	to wade	to walk through deep water
	to make good progress	*here:* to move fast
	current 'kʌrənt	direction in which water flows
	in their favour 'feivə	*here:* helping them
	to glide	to move smoothly
	in sight	to be seen
	shallow 'ʃæləu	not deep
	to drift	to float away

7 The Shelter

26	in places	in parts, here and there
	hand-rail	long piece of wood or metal to hold on to, at the side of the path
	heather 'heðə	plant with purple or white flowers often growing on sandy ground
27	tangled 'tæŋgld	in an unordered mass
	to rustle 'rʌsl	to make a sound like leaves blowing in the wind
	frightening 'fraitniŋ	making you feel afraid
	damp	rather wet
	to run along	*here:* to go from one end to the other
	to gasp gɑːsp	to breathe in quickly with surprise
	in a heap	*here:* in an unnatural position
28	at his touch	when Neil touched him
	to groan	to make the sound of a person in pain

forehead	'fɔrid	part of head between eyes and hair
bruise	bru:z	blue or black mark on the skin
inflamed		*here:* red and swollen
smear	smiə	wet mark
ambulance	'æmbjuləns	car which takes people to hospital

8 Two Pretty Fish

29 receiver		part of telephone which you pick up
to dial	dail	When you telephone, you must first dial the number
999		number to dial if you need police, ambulance etc. quickly
to make use of		to use, to use the help of
to draw up		*here:* to stop
kerb	kə:b	edge of pavement near road
sergeant	'sɑ:dʒənt	*here:* police-officer, one step below an inspector
30 to reassure s.o.	ˌri:ə'ʃuə	to make s.o. feel sure
groundsmen		men who keep ground (*here:* golf course) in order
equipment		tools, things needed for work
lobster	'lɔbstə	sea-animal with eight legs and two claws
lobster-pot		kind of basket used for catching lobsters
31 chubby	'tʃʌbi	rather fat
day-break		sunrise, beginning of the day
puzzled	'pʌzld	not understanding
tiny	'taini	very small
speed-boat		fast motor-boat
to speed		to travel fast
32 scattered		here and there
to nod		*here:* to move one's head in greeting
ray		beam of light
yacht	jɔt	kind of boat

to steer s.th.		to guide, move s.th. in a certain direction
to pick s.o. up		to collect s.o.
I bet		*here:* I expect, I feel sure
to aim		to point gun at what you want to shoot
to go for		to attack
to surge	səːdʒ	to move with sudden force
to compete with	kəm'piːt	*here:* to have a chance against
to make for		to move towards
collision	kə'liʒən	accident when cars, boats etc. hit each other (collide)
33 to duck down		to bend down out of the way
crash		collision, accident, loud noise of this
to lurch	ləːtʃ	to move suddenly to one side
violent	'vaiələnt	wild, uncontrolled
spray		fine drops of water
to splash		(of water) to fall in drops
dismay	dis'mei	fear
to capsize	kæp'saiz	(of boat) to turn over
to flounder about	'flaundə	to move about helplessly
craft	krɑːft	*here:* boat
to swear	swɛə	to use bad language
34 soaking wet	'səukiŋ	very wet
sullen	'sʌlən	angry and silent
station		*here:* police station
to head for		to move towards
her		*here:* the yacht (boats, cars etc. are often called 'she' in English)
dot		small round mark
international waters		part of sea which does not belong to one country
to wipe out		*here:* to destroy

9 The 'Major'

bandage	'bændidʒ	piece of cloth bound round a cut etc.

to ache	eik	to hurt
injury	'indʒəri	damage to part of the body
35 headache		painful, hurting head
to switch off		to turn off
36 to overhear		to hear what other people (who are not talking to you) are saying
dissatisfied		not content, not happy
properly		*here:* clearly, well
vague	veig	unclear
definite	'definit	clear
to make up one's mind		to decide
to emerge	i'mə:dʒ	to come out
37 to grab		to seize
appropriate	ə'prəupriit	fitting, rightly used

10 At the Dinner Table

you bet		*here:* you can be sure of that
38 Goodness!		Good heavens!
stroke		*here:* mark, line
to steal up on s.o.		to come up to s.o. quietly and unnoticed
fugitive	'fju:dʒitiv	person who runs away
safe and sound		unharmed, not hurt
jolly good		very good
Jolly good show!		That's fine!
desperately	'despəritli	*here:* very
clumsy	'klʌmzi	without skill; not moving in the right way
to choke		to cough after eating s.th.
Danish Blue		kind of cheese
awkward	'ɔ:kwəd	clumsy
to bump into		to knock into, to touch by mistake
nasty	'nɑ:sti	unpleasant
the previous night	'pri:vjəs	the night before
to introduce		*here:* to tell you the name of
to camp out		to sleep outside

to do research	ri'sə:tʃ	to try to find out new information about s.th.
39 chambermaid	'tʃeimbəmeid	woman who keeps hotel rooms in order
confident	'kɔnfidənt	sure of oneself, not afraid
from Sue's angle	'æŋgl	as Sue saw it
skipping		half walking, half jumping
clue	klu:	helpful information which may lead to the answer to a problem
to burst out	bə:st	*here:* to say in sudden excitement
to check up on		to find out about
40 loo	lu:	*(coll.)* toilet, lavatory
accounts	ə'kaunts	*here:* money matters, books
decisive	di'saisiv	firm, knowing what one wants

11 The Smuggler's Arms

It gave me the shock of my life!		It was a very great surprise to me
to be mistaken		to be wrong
to confirm s.th.	kən'fə:m	to show that s.th. is true
suspicions	səs'piʃənz	*here:* feelings that s.o. may be a criminal
to cooperate	kəu'ɔpəreit	to help by working together
41 to identify s.o.	ai'dentifai	to say who s.o. is
evidence	'evidəns	information which helps to prove s.th.
to incriminate	in'krimineit	*here:* to give information which involves s.o. in a crime
accomplice	ə'kɔmplis	helper in crime
to give s.o. away		*here:* to tell the police about s.o.
severe	si'viə	hard, serious
case		*here:* criminal affair
gang		group (*here:* of criminals)
drive		private road which leads up to a house or hotel
Sarge		*(slang)* Sergeant
to reverse	ri'və:s	*here:* to go backwards

to storm		to speak angrily
to block		to put s.th. in the way of
to produce		*here:* to take out and show
search warrant	'wɔrənt	paper showing that police are allowed to search s.o.'s house etc.
42 proprietor	prə'praiətə	owner (of hotel, shop etc.)
reluctant	ri'lʌktənt	unwilling
boot		*here:* place in back of car for suitcases etc.
lid		top
slab		*here:* flat four-sided piece
bar of chocolate		wrapped piece of chocolate
43 I shouldn't wonder		It wouldn't surprise me
drawn		*here:* worried-looking
to mimic, mimicked, mimicking	'mimik	*here:* to make one's voice sound like another person's
to roar with laughter	rɔː	to laugh very loudly
Dad		*(coll.)* father
to agree	ə'griː	to say 'yes', to have the same opinion
in the end		after a long time
It's just as well		It's lucky, it's good
to be at sixes and sevens		to be very badly organized
44 to catch up with s.o.		*here:* to catch s.o.
drugs	drʌgz	*here:* general word for hashish, marijuana, opium etc.
any moment		very soon
marvellous		wonderful
advertisement	əd'vəːtismənt	information (often on T.V. or in the paper) that recommends s.th.
to spin a yarn	jɑːn	to tell a story (often about sailors and the sea)